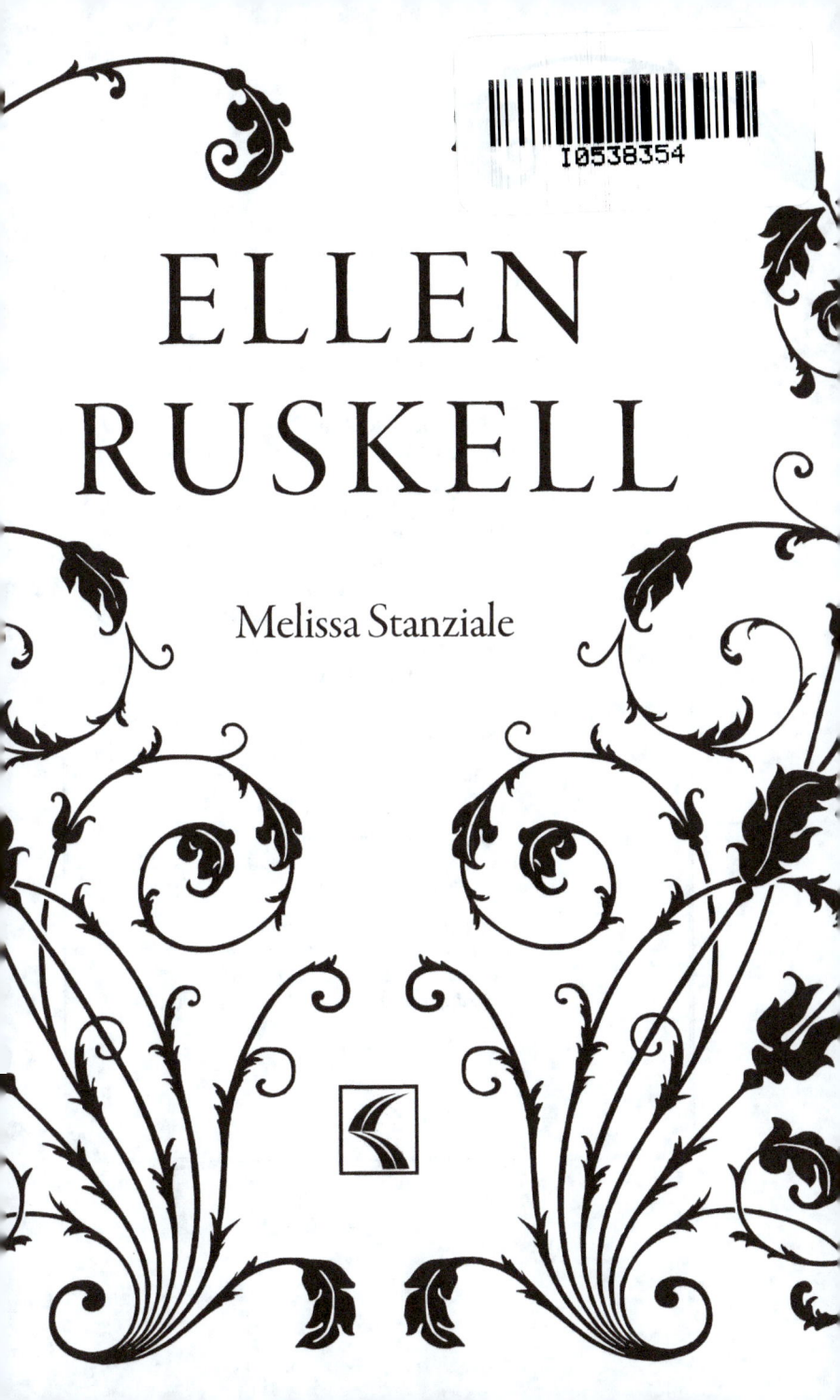

ELLEN RUSKELL

Melissa Stanziale

Produced and printed
by Stillwater River Publications.

Visit our website at
www.StillwaterPress.com
for more information.

First Stillwater River Publications Edition

ISBN: 978-1-952521-98-0

1 2 3 4 5 6 7 8 9 10
Written by Melissa Stanziale
Published by Stillwater River Publications,
Pawtucket, RI, USA.

For my parents,
Priscilla & Giovanni

Mrs. Crowhurst guided me into a lofty oak-paneled library where the master of the house reclined on a couch before the fire. A large white dog lay at his feet. The walls were covered by high oak shelves lined with books, some new and some very old. There were three long black marble tables, one of them covered with piles of books and papers, and behind these were several massive bookshelves. Mr. Lanchester evidently spent a great deal of time in his library.

"Miss Ellen Ruskell, sir," said Mrs. Crowhurst.

He nodded without taking his eyes from the flames and gestured for me to be seated. I placed myself in the chair beside the couch. The dog lifted its head to examine me but quickly lost interest and resumed its nap.

"Leave us," said he to Mrs. Crowhurst, with a wave of his white hand. When she left the room, my stomach began to flutter.

I studied my new employer. His face was slender, pale, and framed by wavy black hair that reached his neck. He was no more than thirty and quite handsome, but there was a hint of malevolence about him. He stared into the fire and must have seen something engaging there, for it was some time before he acknowledged me. When he finally looked up, he appeared to be puzzled, as if he suddenly became aware of my presence and was startled by it. His eyes were icy blue, and he resembled a cruel, beautiful dog eyeing a rodent.

He sneered and looked away. "Your countenance is pleasing, too pleasing," said he, resting his cheek on his hand.

A hot blush spread over my cheeks. "I beg your pardon, sir?"

"You are not plain. Mrs. Crowhurst has failed to accommodate my request for a plain governess. Prettiness is a distraction that I will not tolerate in my house."

My nerves withered. I thought I had secured the position. Was I now to be turned away? "I'm sorry my appearance offends you, Mr. Lanchester, but—"

"It does not offend me." He lifted his head from his hand and looked at me. "On the contrary, it is a remarkably interesting and attractive appearance. But, as I said, I do not wish to be distracted."

"I assure you that my appearance will not interfere with the way I perform my duties. And, as the governess, I expect that most of my time will be spent with my pupil. How much could I possibly see of you?"

"Humph!" said he, crossing his arms over his chest.

I waited anxiously, expecting to be dismissed, until he spoke. "Do you read, Ms. Ruskell?"

I nodded.

"Life is a drab disappointment after closing a book, don't you think?"

"I think that such talk leads to madness."

"Indeed, it does. It drove my sister mad."

It was a strange piece of information to share with a prospective employee. "Reading?"

"Precisely. There was no novelty in her life, so

she sought it in books. The poor, misguided creature. Reading can be rather dangerous."

"Perhaps to an unstable mind." I bit my lip, instantly regretting the remark.

"And do you possess a stable mind, Ms. Ruskell?" he asked, scowling.

"I possess a mind that has endured much."

He turned and looked at me with interest but said nothing.

"Where is she now?" I asked, unable to suppress the question.

"I am weary of this conversation." He closed his eyes, placed his long fingers on both sides of his forehead, and began to rub his temples. "I am sure Mrs. Crowhurst will furnish you with the rest of the story about my sister. Good day, Ms. Ruskell."

"Before I go, sir, I must know if you wish to engage me as governess."

"Very well. I will agree to a trial, provided you are capable. You did come highly recommended by your former employer, this Lady Heatherstone. Now leave me," said he, waving his hand dismissively. He sank into a sullen mood, and I was glad to take leave of him.

❧

"He expressed some dissatisfaction with my appearance."

"Pay him no mind, my dear," said Mrs. Crowhurst, pouring reddish tea from an ivory ceramic pot. "I informed him about your appearance prior to the introduction, but he can be peevish. He occupies his library most of the time, which is a blessing."

I accepted the cup. "He seems unhappy. Do you know why?"

She shrugged. "His disposition is generally not a pleasant one. But it may have something to do with the fact that his father died a few years ago. His brother, Robert, and his wife also died, leaving him with his niece, Alice. Aside from that, there is his mother, Mrs. Lanchester. You will meet them tomorrow."

"I didn't know he had a brother. He mentioned a sister."

"Yes," said she, pouring herself a cup. "He also has a sister."

She grew silent. I was prepared to abandon

the subject when she said, "I suppose you want to know about her?"

"Well, he said you would furnish me with additional information."

"What a terrible man he is," said she, lifting her cup to her lips and attempting to suppress a smile. "Her name is Elsa, and I assume he told you that she is mad."

"Yes, he did. I was surprised he would share such a thing with a stranger."

"William Lanchester will tell anyone who will listen, my dear. Misery knows no discretion, or, at least *his* does not."

Yes, I thought, *his* does not. Why should a miserable man force himself to endure a secret alone when he can burden others with it?

I took a sip of tea and licked my lips. "Is she really mad?"

Mrs. Crowhurst hesitated. She looked into the fire as if seeking advice from the flames on how to respond. "Yes," said she, finally. "Quite mad."

"Where is she?"

"She lives in the East Wing. Do not worry, my dear, you will never see her."

I leaned back in my chair and stared at the fire,

also seeking answers and finding none. "How very sad."

The next morning, I joined Mrs. Crowhurst in the dining room. It was a handsome room with red brocade walls covered with gilt-framed paintings of long-dead ancestors. A long mahogany table was at the center and standing at one end, opposite the entrance, was Mrs. Crowhurst dressed in a black silk gown. She was giving instructions to one of the maids. A frail elderly woman in a grey dress was seated at the head of the table; she looked at me and smiled, or at least attempted to smile, and then lowered her eyes. Mrs. Crowhurst gestured for me to enter. She sat in the seat to the left of the old woman, and I sat to the right. It was a great relief not to find the master of the house at table.

"Mrs. Lanchester," Mrs. Crowhurst began, "this is Miss Ellen Ruskell. She is the new governess."

The old woman looked at me; the ghost of a smile haunted her withered lips and vanished. "It is nice to make your acquaintance, my dear."

I returned the greeting. She was a resigned old

woman, perhaps in her early seventies, and not interested in anything beyond a cup of tea. From time to time, she nodded in vague acknowledgement of what Mrs. Crowhurst said, but for the most part she seemed distant and detached. After a short time, she stood up, said good morning, and left us.

"Please forgive her, Ms. Ruskell, she is a retiring woman with very delicate health."

"I understand completely," I said with a dismissive wave of my hand.

Mrs. Crowhurst smiled, evidently appreciative of my tolerance.

"Shall I have the pleasure of meeting Miss Lanchester today?" I asked, wondering why she was not present.

She seated herself. "Yes, of course. I will take you to her when we are finished here. I think you will find her a most agreeable pupil."

"Yes, I'm sure. What are her accomplishments?"

"I'm afraid you will find Alice a bit behind in her studies," said she, with a sad smile. "As I said, her parents died a year ago, and she has been through a great deal."

"Then I will not overtax her, but I do look forward to helping her catch up."

"And I'm sure you are most capable of helping her do so. I told her that you are a true lady with many accomplishments."

"Mr. Lanchester did not ask any questions about my previous experience or qualifications."

"No and he will not. He has little interest in his niece or anything else that does not affect him directly. You will be glad to know that he will not interfere with your work like some meddling mamma." She smiled again. It was not an attractive smile; it looked rather ugly when her lips spread across her small, sour face. I thought the pointed corners of her mouth might somehow venture beyond its withered borders. But, despite the hideous expression, she was my only friend in an unfamiliar place, and I did not dislike her. In fact, I was reassured by what she told me. Since I had no desire to spend any more time with Mr. Lanchester, I was content with Mrs. Crowhurst's companionship.

❧

After breakfast, Mrs. Crowhurst brought me to Alice's room, which was at the back of the house.

When we entered, she was sitting up in bed. Her only companions were the doll at her side and a brown and white cat napping at the edge of the bed. She was a pale little phantom with blond hair and black eyes. Her features were delicate, and she looked very small in an ordinary-sized bed. The furnishings of the room were sparse, which was a sensible choice for an ailing child, but it gave one a cold, vacant feeling. I pitied the poor little girl who had to pass so many hours there. A small table and chair had been placed near the bed for me, as well as a chalkboard. There were books, some paper, and a quill on the table. Mrs. Crowhurst introduced us and took leave to attend to her household duties.

I noticed two thick books, containing marks, on the table beside the bed. "You like to read, Alice?"

"Yes, ma'am."

"I'm surprised your uncle allows you to read," said I, without thinking.

"Why ma'am?"

"Well, because of…never mind. Forgive me."

"You mean because of my aunt Elsa?"

"Well, yes."

"I would go mad without the books, ma'am, not with them."

What a clever child, I thought. She put me at ease at once, and I seated myself at the table to examine the books and decide where to begin. Mrs. Crowhurst said Alice was behind, so I did not want to embarrass her. But I had to inquire about some of her abilities. "Have you any French?"

"No, Miss."

"Then we will begin with that."

Mrs. Crowhurst was correct—Alice was an agreeable pupil. She was focused and ambitious in her studies, particularly with foreign languages. Nonetheless I did not want to strain her; so, after we had practiced for a while and she had made good progress, I insisted that she rest. When I was about to leave her room, I heard footsteps in the hall. I opened the door, expecting to find Mrs. Crowhurst there, but she was not. A veiled figure in white glided past me and turned the corner at the end of the hall. I suddenly felt as if I was alone in a churchyard at dusk.

"What is it?" Alice called from her bed.

"I saw someone, a woman in a white dress."

"Oh, that is Aunt Elsa."

"I thought she was confined to the East Wing."

"She is, but sometimes she wanders about the house. You should make mention of it to Mrs. Crowhurst."

❧

I was on my way downstairs when Mrs. Crowhurst appeared at the bottom of the staircase, holding my black shawl. "Your morning lessons are finished now, I suppose?" she asked.

"Yes. Alice did very well. I'm pleased with her. There is something I would like to tell you. I saw—"

"I am so glad to hear it, my dear. We can discuss whatever you like later. Mr. Lanchester has requested that you accompany him on a walk through the grounds."

"He has?" I placed a hand upon my suddenly nervous stomach. "You said he never leaves the library."

"Indeed it is rare for him to leave it, but for some reason he wants to venture out today, and he craves some society. Please do oblige him. He is waiting outside at the front of the house."

I did not relish the idea of an afternoon walk with the master. What if he asked questions, probing questions that I did not care to answer? "Of course." I took the shawl from her and wrapped it around myself.

Mr. Lanchester was on the front lawn not far from the house. He was seated at a small table with his mother, waiting for me to emerge no doubt. His white dog sat close by, obedient and content. When he saw me, he stood up and the sun shone brightly upon him, a slender figure in a dark suit. He lifted a hand to his forehead to shield his delicate blue eyes from the sunlight and gazed upon me. When I stood before him, the left corner of his mouth curled slightly, but he would not permit it to form a smile.

"Good afternoon, Ms. Ruskell."

"Good afternoon, sir. Mrs. Crowhurst told me—"

"Yes, I desire some company. Walk with me. I will see you in a while, Mother. See that you don't excite yourself." He sprang up and gestured for me to follow him.

It surprised me when he uttered this command because I could not imagine Mrs. Lanchester in a state of excitement. We were not far away when I looked back at the lonely figure seated at the table. She was not looking at us; she stared blankly upon her son's vast demesne and gave no indication that she was impressed by it. Indeed, it appeared that nothing, not even the magnificent view, could rouse her from her mood of dreary silence.

"Is your mother unwell?" I asked.

"No, she is quite well today, all things considered."

I did not dare to inquire what those "things" might be and changed the subject.

"What a magnificent park!" I cried as we walked on the green sloping lawn; for it had been some time since I had seen such verdure.

"Yes, it is, isn't it? My family has lived here for many generations."

I nervously sought a reply. "I was sorry to hear about the deaths of your family members."

"Thank you, but I do not want to discuss that."

"What would you like to discuss?"

"I would like to discuss you, Ms. Ruskell."

My cheeks began to burn. "The sun is so very bright and hot. Can we find a shaded spot?"

"Certainly."

And what will you do once the shaded spot is found? I asked myself. Once he begins to ask questions you cannot answer, he will see that he has a deceptive individual in his employ.

We entered upon an avenue shaded by beech trees and he began his interrogation. "Tell me of your former employer, Lady Heatherstone."

"She was exceedingly kind to me. We were devoted to each other."

"Then why did you leave? Surely that was an ideal situation."

"Because her daughter died, and there was no longer any reason for me to stay." I kept my eyes on the ground.

"How sad. How old was the child?"

"She was seven years old."

"I don't believe you," said he.

"I beg your pardon?"

"You heard me, Ms. Ruskell. I don't believe you."

"You have no reason not to believe me, sir."

"Don't I? I barely know you."

"I have furnished you with my references and, as a new employer, you should require nothing more." I turned to leave, and he stretched his arm out in front of me, his hand touching the trunk of a nearby tree. I panicked, recalling how Lord Heatherstone's long arm had barred the doorway of my bedroom.

"What the deuce do I care about references?" he hissed. "I know you are hiding something, Ms. Ruskell."

His face was very close to mine. I stared into his icy blue eyes, attempting to burn them in their sockets with my fiery rage. It was the same way I looked into Lord Heatherstone's fat, white face when he forbade me to leave.

"Beautiful women often have something to hide. And you, with your hair as black as sin and your eyes as green as absinthe, most certainly fall into that category. Now tell me the real reason you left your former situation."

There was some part of me that wanted to reveal the truth to him, to anyone. A secret can be a heavy burden, especially for a woman who is alone. Despite my anger and revulsion for him, the truth began to erupt: "It was…I could not…I could not endure the situation any longer. I could not live that way!"

An arrogant smirk crept over his pearl-white lips. "I see."

The two words conveyed the judgement he passed, which was that I had compromised myself at my former post. You are a fool, Ellen! I thought. Why would this stupid, hollow man have any sympathy for you? He was silent for a few moments, standing there with an asinine grin on his face.

"Tell me, Ms. Ruskell, was it the Lady's husband?"

"No, it was not. You do not understand."

"I think I understand perfectly."

"You understand nothing."

"I understand the ways of the world. And you are a worldly woman, no doubt."

I began to back away from him. "Do not come any closer."

The next moment my back was against a tree. I pressed myself into its coarse, uneven surface in an attempt to create distance between myself and my oppressor; his face was alarmingly close. I watched his lips as he spoke, and I could see his white teeth, and his moist, red tongue. It was a more appealing sight than Lord Heatherstone's greedy, slobbering maw, but I still did not desire it.

"You bewitched her husband, did you not? And when the Lady learned of it, she dismissed you."

I shook my head. "No, no. That is not what happened."

He licked his lips and began to lower them toward mine. Those lips would have silenced my protests if I had not struck him.

He stared at me in surprise, holding one hand against the assaulted cheek. It took a moment for him to digest what had occurred. "Forgive me, Ms. Ruskell," said he, recovering quickly with another smug grin. "This is why I prefer not to be distracted."

I shoved him aside. "You think because I am a woman in your employ that you can take such liberties? You are mistaken, sir, in more ways than one!" I spat and stomped off.

❧

When I came stomping into the house, Mrs. Crowhurst asked what was wrong. I told her I was ill and retreated to my room. Trembling all over, I laid myself on the four-poster bed and tried to think of how to proceed. Could I remain here? Lanchester was dangerously perceptive, and it would not be long before he discovered the truth. Even if I could stay, what if he made further advances? I could not—would not—endure that. I wanted a secure, respectable situation. My head ached; my temples were throbbing. I lay there for a quarter of an hour, shivering and staring at the dark hearth, wishing one of the servants would appear to light it. I closed my eyes.

The door opened, and I heard the determined steps of Mrs. Crowhurst. A tray was placed gently on the table near the bed. There were other steps as well—those of a servant—who entered the room, most likely one of the maids, who busied herself with lighting a fire. The servant left, but Mrs. Crowhurst lingered. What was she doing? She approached the bed; the rustling of her silk skirts was sinister at that proximity. She was so close that a hint of her strange perfume invaded my nostrils, causing them to twitch. The only sounds were my rapid breathing and the crackling of the fresh fire. I imagined her extending her long silk-clad arm, reaching out with her bony hand, her long wrinkled fingers hovering over my body, and I shivered. I envied her ability to repulse. If only I could repel others, particularly predatory men, in the same way. *Share your power with me, dark witch,*

I pleaded with this grotesque goddess of night. When I opened my eyes, I was alone.

I took a few sips of the tea that had been left for me but had no appetite for the assorted viands on the tray. I sat by the fire for a while, attempting to read a book of German ghost stories, but it was no use. It seemed that I should do something, but what? Seek out Mrs. Crowhurst and tell her that the master had taken a liberty? What could she do except advise me to overlook it? And what if she thought I had encouraged such attention from him? It would not be wise to jeopardize her opinion of me and, ultimately, my situation. There was nowhere else to go, and the thought of advertising again was distasteful.

But would Mr. Lanchester permit me to stay after that episode? I was justified in striking him, but that meant nothing. He was the master and my employer. I was just a governess, a helpless dependent who could do nothing but hope that she would not be dismissed. If he allowed me to stay, it would not be possible to avoid his company, especially if he requested mine. How could

I explain my aversion to him to Mrs. Crowhurst? She already suspected something. I would have to conceal it. In the course of one afternoon, I had created another burdensome secret.

I almost surrendered to my bed once again, but the sound of footsteps in the hall aroused me. They were familiar, hurried footsteps. I ran to the door, flung it open, and peered into the hall. Again, I saw the veiled figure turning the corner at the end of the corridor. This time I pursued her. Of course, I did not know how to confront a mad woman, but that did not prevent me from following her.

I followed the ghostly streak of white through the labyrinthine corridors—she was always just out of my reach—until she turned into the main hall. Before I reached the hall, I heard a door open and close; she had gone into the East Wing. I crossed the flagstone floor of the magnificent hall hung with medieval tapestries and approached the door; the knob was cold in my hand. Surprisingly, it was unlocked.

The gloomy East Wing stretched before me. The dim light of the fading afternoon allowed me to see the tall windows dressed in heavy drapes on the left and several doors with fireplaces between them on the right. The raw coldness of the corridor informed me that those drapes were never parted to admit the sun, and those fireplaces had not been lit in ages. I walked quickly and then ran down the hall, which would soon be a maw of darkness.

I tried every door and found them all locked, except for the last one at the end of the hall, which opened into an empty room—the room of Elsa Lanchester. It was not the sort of room that would have aligned with the tastes of a lady of Ms. Lanchester's station, but no doubt it had been stripped of many luxuries because of her illness. There was a four-poster bed, a small bookshelf, a threadbare carpet, and a table littered with books and papers. There was also a small fireplace with a bare mantel (except for two burning candles) and an oval portrait of a young woman hung above it. I lifted one of the candles and seated myself at the table where I found a yellowish piece of paper with a quill laid beside it. Some ink had dripped off the tip of the quill and dried long ago. The paper was dated two years ago:

September 9, 1847
    My life is not what I thought it would be. As a girl I spent countless hours reading novels that led

me to believe my own life would reflect their scenes of passion and excitement. Passion and excitement continue to elude me, especially now that I am ill. According to William, I must remain in the East Wing and not excite myself. He believes that my mind has been contaminated by reading and, although I begged him not to take my books away, he had them removed. I managed to hide the works of Mrs. Radcliffe (I could not do without them) and Mrs. Shelley's Frankenstein, *which I began today.*

William says that it is best for me to be confined until my nervous fits subside, but I believe confinement worsens my condition. The longer I am isolated, the more nervous and distracted I become. It is agony to live without stimulation. I would leave this place if I could, but that is impossible. Even if I could escape, how would I survive? A woman alone with no means of support and no male protector would not fare well in the outside world. The only escape from this dreary existence would be to marry some insipid young man of my brother's choosing. I could not bear that; I will not bear that.

I lifted one of the candles and walked to the portrait. Her face was a white oval with long red hair erupting from the crown of her head like lava. Two perfect black arches curved over a pair of crystal blue eyes. She wore a pale blue gown and was seated on a divan, looking off in another direction, detached and inaccessible; she had not connected with the painter who captured her image, and she would not connect with anyone who beheld it afterward.

"Who are you, Elsa Lanchester?" I whispered.

I had never met this woman, but I felt that our sufferings were similar. I knew what it was to have a man's will imposed upon me. In fact, I knew more about it than she ever did, but that did not make her suffering any less significant.

I wanted to know more about Elsa. Had she really gone mad from reading novels? Had the confinement made her condition worse? I cannot explain why I wanted to know about the mad, frenzied spirit who haunted the halls of her brother's house. Perhaps the exercise of trying to discover something served as a distraction from my own predicament. Perhaps I thought it was possible to save her and, in doing so, salvage the ruin of my own life. Perhaps there was simply nothing else to do. It was all these things, I suppose, and none of them.

ॐ

The days were long, but they were filled with work and some pleasure; they passed quietly. I became especially fond of Alice; she was obedient and focused on her studies. The two of us spent many happy hours together in her little bedroom. She was a pleasure to instruct, and her presence was a soothing salve.

There was no outward change in Mrs. Crowhurst's manner toward me, but I felt that she had become slightly reserved. She was not as willing to divulge information about the Lanchester family as she once had been. I suspected that Mr. Lanchester had told her his own version about what occurred in the park and this made her wary of me. It pained me to think that she should harbor such an opinion of me, but I had to accept it. Thankfully, Mr. Lanchester maintained his distance; we rarely saw each other except to pass one another in the hall. His only gesture of acknowledgement was a cold nod, and I reciprocated with an equally frigid inclination of my head.

One morning Mrs. Crowhurst informed me

that Alice was ill and would not be able to study. I was disappointed because our morning lessons were the most pleasant part of my day. Being left with no occupation, I asked Mrs. Crowhurst if she had any task that needed doing. She said she did not and advised me to spend the day at my leisure.

We dined early that night. Mrs. Crowhurst invited me to her parlor afterward, but I complained of tiredness and declined. Thankful to be alone in my bedroom, I undressed and sat before the fire until my eyes grew heavy. The bedclothes were comfortably cold when I settled in and blew out the candle. I closed my eyes and surrendered to peaceful slumber.

I awoke during the night to the sound of low sighing and realized that someone was standing beside my bed. I turned over and saw the veiled figure in white.

"Elsa," I whispered, extending my hand to her.

She stood motionless for a moment, perhaps trying to comprehend that I was pleased to see her. It must have been some time since anyone expressed pleasure at seeing the poor creature. She sat down beside me.

"I hoped you would come, Elsa." I placed my hand upon hers and we sat there in silence for some time.

How can I explain that this mad woman's presence was a balm? I should have been terrified of this figure in white, half shrouded in shadows with her face behind a ghostly veil. I should have screamed because a deranged woman sat by my side in the darkness, but I caressed her hand instead. I was tranquil in her presence, knowing that the living mystery was in my grasp.

"Will you show me your face, Elsa?" I whispered.

She began to lift her veil, revealing her white mouth and then stopped. She pulled it down in a violent gesture that seemed to say you will never see me and, in an instant, she was on her feet, flying to the bedroom door.

"Elsa!" I shouted, throwing the bedclothes aside.

She flung the door open and started down the hall. I followed her through the dark corridors, striving to overtake her before she reached the East Wing, but I failed. She rushed across the great hall, opened the door, and slammed it behind her. I grasped the handle and twisted it with all my strength, but it was locked, and I was divided from her once again.

"Elsa!" I shouted, pounding on the door. "Let me in!"

I carried on in this manner until Mrs. Crowhurst and two maids appeared at the opposite end of the hall. Mrs. Crowhurst was an eerie figure in her long black dressing gown, carrying a silver candelabra with five candles burning in its sconces. The maids, in their plain white gowns and slippers, stood on either side of her like two silly sentinels with terrified expressions on their faces. I disregarded them and continued to strike the door and shout.

"Ellen," said Mrs. Crowhurst.

I turned and faced her. "What do you want?"

She handed the candelabra to one of the maids and approached me. "Come away from the door."

"I will do no such thing," said I, fiercely. "I refuse to leave this spot until I have seen Elsa."

Mrs. Crowhurst looked at me with pity. She was silent for a moment and then spoke. "I am sorry, my dear, but there is no Elsa."

"What?"

"There is no Elsa Lanchester."

Six hands were laid upon me as I fell fainting to the flagstone floor.

I rose late in the afternoon the next day. One of the maids came bearing a tray of food and a request from Mrs. Crowhurst for me to present myself in the library. I dressed quickly and proceeded to that room. Mrs. Crowhurst was seated on the couch before the fire.

"Please sit down, Ms. Ruskell," said she, gesturing toward a chair near the couch.

I placed myself in the chair and folded my hands in my lap, bracing myself for whatever I might hear.

"I trust you are feeling better, my dear," said she, smiling. "You were very upset when we found you last night."

I ignored her inquiry about my health and demanded to know what was going on.

"Very well. I will tell you. Where should I begin?"

"You can begin with Elsa. Why did you say that she does not exist?"

"Because it is true."

"Then who is the woman wandering about this house dressed in a white gown?"

She turned to the back entrance of the library and the figure in white entered, coming toward me. She stood beside my chair, silent and motion-less. I stood up and faced her, the living, breathing mystery. When I lifted the veil, I saw the face of Mr. Lanchester. It was a horror to behold his mas-culine features framed by white lace.

"You despicable man!" said I, tearing the veil off his head.

"Please, Ms. Ruskell, allow me to explain."

"Yes, you shall explain, sir!" said I, violently tossing the veil aside.

He hesitated. Perhaps he was taken aback by my fury. "You should sit down and calm yourself."

"I will stand. Get on with it."

"My sister Elsa died a year ago. In a fit of rage and madness, she flung herself off the roof. Her death was handled quietly because I did not want my mother to know about it. As you know, her health is delicate. I have impersonated my dead sister for this past year to spare Mother the pain of learning that her only daughter is no more. If I did not do so, the shock would have killed her."

I stared at him in disbelief. "This is madness!"

"You may call it madness, Ms. Ruskell, but it was all I could think of to do to preserve my moth-er's life in her fragile state."

"Why did you visit me disguised as Elsa?"

Those fierce, wintry blue eyes looked into my depths. "I knew that you were repulsed by me after what happened, so I took the liberty of visiting you as Elsa. It was the only way you would permit me to come near you."

I turned from him in disgust. "I will leave this place at once," said I, starting for the door in livid strides.

"Where will you go, Ellen?" he asked.

I stopped. The question pulled me back like a short leash pulling back a mad dog. Indeed, where would I go?

"Are we the only ones who have been deceptive?" His tone changed from contrite to snide. "My contacts have recently informed me that Lady Heatherstone has been missing these two months. What do you have to say about that?"

I was crippled by consternation, standing there motionless with my back to him and Mrs. Crowhurst.

"You are Lady Heatherstone, aren't you?"

At that moment, I was not sure who I was. A governess? A lady? A desperate woman with few choices? The time had come to decide upon one.

"Yes, I am Lady Heatherstone," I admitted, turning around.

"Why did you come here, my Lady?" asked Mrs. Crowhurst.

"I came here because…my husband, Lord Heatherstone, became involved with another woman."

"I see. And you could not bear it?"

"No, that is not the reason. I never loved him. I loathed him; he is a fat, despicable tyrant. When he became involved with this other woman, I knew he would seek some way to rid himself of me, so I fled."

"And you had a child who died?"

"Yes, my daughter, Clara, died a year ago. The governess—Ms. Cowles—stayed on even though there was no need for her to do so."

Silence fell over us. At last, they knew my secret, and I was relieved at having unburdened myself.

"And what will you do now, Lady Heatherstone?" asked Mr. Lanchester.

I walked back to the armchair in defeat and placed myself in it, sinking into its comfortable recesses. "I have no idea."

Mr. Lanchester kneeled before me. "Stay here

with us," said he, looking eagerly into my face.

I closed my eyes and quietly absorbed the idea. "I could not possibly do that."

"Why not? Alice adores you, and she is still in need of a governess. You would have honest work and a salary to go with it. Mrs. Crowhurst is also very fond of you. You would be a great help to her. I'm sure my mother would also be pleased if you stay. And I will not interfere with you in the least. You have my word."

I kept my eyes closed and turned the idea over in my mind, wondering what this man's word was worth. I had no desire to see his hopeful face looking back at me, so I kept my eyes closed, and the darkness was a comfortable, albeit temporary, escape from my predicament. I had nowhere else to go and, despite the bizarre circumstances, it was a comfortable and secure place. The child was a delight, and I enjoyed instructing her. Mrs. Crowhurst had been a pleasant companion to me, and his mother was a harmless old woman. They were not impediments, but I was not such a fool to believe that Mr. Lanchester could contain his passion. He would relent for some time and maintain his distance, but after a while his desire would get the best of him. He would make another attempt and what would I do then? Another rejection would infuriate him. Even if I could have returned his love—which I could not—I was still married and not free to bestow my affection on anyone.

"Well, what do you say Lady Heatherstone?" he asked.

I opened my eyes and was about to speak when one of the maids entered. "I beg your pardon, Mr. Lanchester, but there is a Lord Heatherstone here to see you."

After a moment's hesitation, Mr. Lanchester replied, "Very well. I will see him in a few moments."

"I will not go back with him," I said, not waiting for the question to be put to me.

"I am glad to hear it," said Mr. Lanchester, his blue eyes sparkling. "Then we must rid ourselves of him for good."

I nodded and held out my hand. "Give me the dress."

❧

I stood among the shadows, hiding behind a bookcase at the back of the library.

Mrs. Crowhurst marched into the library followed by my tall, portly husband. "Here is Lord Heatherstone." After making her announcement, she left the room without looking back.

"Good evening, Mr. Lanchester," said he with a bow. "I am Lord Henry Heatherstone, and I have reason to believe that my wife, Lady Elizabeth, is here. I have come for her."

"May I inquire, Your Lordship, as to why you seek your wife here on my estate?"

"Don't trifle with me, Mr. Lanchester," said he, boldly. "I know she is here."

"Very well. You are quite right. She has been with us some time, passing herself off as a governess." Mr. Lanchester smiled mischievously after relaying this piece of information that did not please my husband.

"I see," he replied with a dour expression. "I have come to collect her. If you will kindly summon her, we will be on our way."

"As you wish," said Mr. Lanchester, nonchalantly. "Please come forward, Lady Elizabeth."

I emerged from the back entrance of the library wearing the vacant expression of a madwoman and placed myself on the couch. Henry was aghast at the sight of his wife, dumb and deranged, shuffling into the room dressed in an old white gown.

"What is this?" he asked, outraged.

"This is your wife, Lord Heatherstone. As you can see, her senses have taken leave of her. I believe she endured some hardship while living with you. She told me it was a matter of another woman."

"There was no other woman. My wife was excessively jealous of any woman I paid the slightest attention to." It took great effort for me to remain silent and listen to his infernal mendacity.

"May I ask if there were any particular women in the household who your attentions were focused on?"

My husband scowled. "No, indeed, there were not. I was merely friendly toward our governess, Ms. Cowles, and my wife imagined that a romantic attachment had formed between us."

Mr. Lanchester grinned and said, "How strange that she should envy an employer's friendliness toward his employee. Indeed, it affected her so deeply that she abandoned you."

My husband stared hard at Lanchester with his dark brows drawn together.

"Surely," continued Mr. Lanchester, "a husband

would not discard his wife for the governess, would he, Lord Heatherstone?"

At this my corpulent husband seized Mr. Lanchester's collar. He pulled him forward; their faces were inches apart. "What I do in my own house is none of your business, sir!" He snarled. "Now I will take this confounded slut and be on my way."

Mr. Lanchester raised one of his black eyebrows in a dangerous arch, grasped the lord's hands, and pushed him. I was impressed by the push, which must have taken considerable strength. Lord Heatherstone stumbled across the room and, with some effort, shifted his girth in order to regain balance. He glared at Mr. Lanchester, his face fixed in an angry scowl.

"I will murder you, sir," Mr. Lanchester said, walking toward my husband with a dark expression on his face.

My husband steadied himself and, discerning the ferocity of his opponent, his expression softened. "Please, sir, let us not resort to violence."

Mr. Lanchester approached him and, coming very closely to his fat face, whispered, "Get out."

"What of my wife?"

"Leave her here and return to your mistress. I'm sure you will find that arrangement satisfactory."

"Leave her here?" my husband asked in astonishment.

"Precisely. Let people believe she is dead. I assume very few know of her disappearance, and I am sure you can arrange a false death."

"Why on earth would you want to keep her here?"

Mr. Lanchester hesitated; it was difficult to produce a plausible explanation, and I could not assist him. He responded with a vague, dismissive statement. "Don't question me, Lord Heatherstone. My reasons for what I do are my own, and I will not discuss them."

My husband glanced at me and then at Mr. Lanchester. I knew that his greedy, gluttonous mind was trying to determine which course would be most favorable. Finally, he decided that it was best to allow this eccentric stranger to take his mad wife off his hands and never trouble himself over the matter again. He licked his thick white lips and produced a handkerchief from his coat pocket.

"I suppose," said he, patting his moist forehead with the handkerchief, "that it could be arranged.

What payment do you require for keeping her here?"

Mr. Lanchester was disgusted by the question. "No payment is required," he said. "I only ask that you never seek out your wife again. And never return here."

My husband nodded nervously. "Very well."

He looked at me once before taking his leave, but there was no tenderness in his expression. It was a look of concern that I—his lunatic wife— should be contained and never disturb him and his precious mistress.

❧

When my husband left, Mr. Lanchester and I were alone in the library. Although my husband had not been my protector, I suddenly felt a chill at the idea of being completely at the mercy of Mr. Lanchester. That stupid, arrogant grin crept across his face.

"There, you are free, my dear," said Lanchester, walking toward me.

"I prefer to be called Ellen," I responded, backing away from him.

I felt anything but free as he came toward me with that sinister grin. His expression was expectant and seemed to say *aren't you grateful to me*? He sensed my discomfort, and, with some effort, he looked away. He forced the smirk off his face and replaced it with a gentle, patient expression.

"Very well then, Ellen. I am pleased that you have decided to stay. Perhaps, in time, you will also be pleased and—"

"No, I will not. Please stop walking toward me."

He stopped and, for an instant, a hurt expression crossed his features, but he recovered quickly, assuming his usual air of confidence.

"You never know, Ms. Ruskell. Sometimes we harbor desires that we keep secret from ourselves."

"The only desire I have, Mr. Lanchester, is to be left alone."

"Well, I gave my word that I will not interfere with you. I will leave you to yourself. Feel free to remain in the library for as long as you wish."

With that he turned and left the room, leaving me in peace and silence. I threw myself on the sofa and, sitting forward, placed my face in my hands.

Well, I thought, one must always endure something, but one should at least be able to choose what she will endure, and I had made my choice. But what would I do during that time beside mourn the loss of Elsa Lanchester? I sat there, drowning in dreary thoughts, for hours. The house had grown dark and silent; the others had gone to bed. I stood up to light a few candles and returned to my seat. After some time, I began to feel cold and hugged myself, trying to resist the chill, but it was no use; it soon became unbearably cold.

I stared into space and concentrated until a dim outline began to materialize in the candlelight. Gradually, a transparent figure came into focus. She (it was a woman or had once been a woman) stood before me with a mane of long, disheveled hair hanging down each side of her breast. The features of her wasted face were heavy with sadness and disappointment. She was dressed in a ragged shroud. Perhaps you think I was afraid, recoiling in terror at the specter before me? I was not. There is no explanation for the absence of fear in the presence of a phantom, but I was as silent and serene as snow falling at midnight.

"Elsa," I said, standing. "I'm so very glad you're here."

"Remain seated," she answered in an echoing voice.

I lowered myself to the couch and waited. She walked to the opposite chair, dragging the train of her shroud, and seated herself. As I sat there staring at my ghostly visitor, I recalled something from a novel I had read: the dead often return to ask a living person to avenge them. Was that why she had come?

"Is there something you would like me to do for you?" I asked.

"Nothing can be done for the dead."

"Then…why have you come?"

"To warn you. You must not remain here," was her response.

"I assure you I have no wish to remain here, but where else can I go at present?"

She looked off to the side, a sad, dejected look, and sighed. When she lifted her head and faced me, she said, "Reflect on your experience and record it."

I was astonished to receive this advice. "You mean write down what has happened? Who would want to hear my story?"

"The story is as much mine as it is yours."

"Sad ghost, you ask too much of me! I do not have the will to write."

She raised a white hand to silence me. "All who live have a will (and even some who are dead). Do not raise these objections. There is no time. You must do as I advise." She began to flicker like a white, haunted flame that is about to go out. "Go now. You have much to do." She faded slowly into the darkness until the chair was vacant.

I was alone again.

I sat there, completely astonished, and considered the ghost's decree. I thought of all that I had been in my life thus far: a wife, a mother, a governess, and a madwoman. But I had never been an author. Those former selves were haunted by a sinister sameness, but here was an opportunity to be something—someone—new. Did I dare to seize it? If I wrote the story—mine and Elsa's—then I could attempt to have it published and earn my bread in a new way, a way that would enable me to leave and go wherever I wished.

I stood up, took two candles in their tapers, and went to one of the tables. There I found paper, books, a quill, and an inkstand. I arranged Lanchester's books in a pile and put them to one side. After this, I examined the papers, looking for whatever blank sheets I could find. Once an adequate supply had been found, I seized the writing instrument and thought back to the beginning.

I began writing: "Mrs. Crowhurst guided me into a lofty oak-paneled library...." There was some hesitation, and then the words came so fast I could scarcely catch them with my pen.

I was interrupted when the library door crept open, and Mrs. Crowhurst entered with the intrusive light of her candelabra. Unwilling to be disturbed, I did not look up and continued to write.

"It is very late, Ellen," she whispered. "Would you like to retire?"

"No, I would not. Go now. I have much to do."

THE END